A TEMPLAR BOOK

Produced by The Templar Company plc,
Pippbrook Mill, London Road, Dorking, Surrey RH4 1JE, Great Britain.

Text copyright © *The Enchanted Doll* 1926-1953 by Darrell Waters Limited
Illustration and design copyright © 1994 by The Templar Company plc
Enid Blyton is a registered trademark of Darrell Waters Limited

This edition produced for Parragon Books,
Unit 13-17, Avonbridge Trading Estate, Atlantic Road, Avonmouth, Bristol BS11 9QD

This book contains material first published as
The Enchanted Doll in Enid Blyton's Sunny Stories
and Sunny Stories between 1926 and 1953.

Illustrated by Maggie Downer

Printed and bound in Italy

ISBN 1 85813 533 8

Enid Blyton's

POCKET LIBRARY

THE ENCHANTED DOLL

Illustrated by Maggie Downer

PARRAGON

Anna had a pretty doll called Victoria whom she loved very much indeed. The only thing she wished was that Victoria could walk and talk, instead of just lying or sitting perfectly still, staring at Anna with her wide-open blue eyes.

"I can pretend you talk to me, and I can pretend you run about and play," said Anna. "But you don't really and truly – and it *would* be such fun if just for once you would really come alive!"

Anna felt quite certain that if only she *could* walk and talk, she would make her a wonderful friend, for Anna had no brothers or sisters, so she was often lonely. That was why she played so much with Victoria. But Victoria just sat and stared, and didn't move a finger or say a word!

Then one day a very strange thing happened when Anna took Victoria for a walk in Pixie Wood. Although it had such a lovely name, Anna had never seen any pixies or anything at all exciting in Pixie Wood. It was just like an ordinary wood.

But today it seemed a little different. The trees seemed closer together, as if they were nodding and whispering to one another. The sun couldn't get in between the branches, and the wood was dark and rather mysterious. Anna took Victoria by the hand and walked her over the grass, talking to her. Her doll's pram was broken and had gone to be mended, which was why Victoria was not riding in it as usual.

Anna walked on through the wood and then stopped suddenly in surprise. In front of her stood a tiny pram, a little smaller than a doll's pram, and it shone like pure gold. It had a little white hood with a silver fringe, and the pram cover was white too, with gold embroidery on it.

"Whatever is a doll's pram doing here?" wondered Anna, for she knew there were no other children about.

Anna went over to the pram and turned back the cover. There was no doll inside – but would you believe it, there was a little bottle full of milk!

"But this pram can't belong to a *real* baby!" cried Anna in astonishment. "It's far too small. Oh! Goodness me! It might belong to a pixie baby!"

"Who's there?" she called.
There was no answer – so
Anna left the pram and ran
to the tree to see if there
really was a pixie peeping
there. But there was no
one at all except a
scurrying rabbit with
a white bobtail!

Anna turned back and was amazed to see the pram running away! It was wheeling off all by itself, between the trees, as fast as ever it could!

"Come back, come back!" shouted Anna. "Oh, please, pram, do come back! Don't take Victoria away!" She ran after the pram as fast as she could, shouting as she went. The pram went faster and faster. It turned a corner by some thick bushes, and disappeared from sight.

Anna ran wildly about, and began to cry when she could not see the pram anywhere.

"Where have you gone, Victoria?" she shouted.

But there was no answer. Victoria had disappeared with the pram. Anna sat down and cried bitterly.

Presently she felt a little hand on her shoulder
and a high, twittering voice said: "What's the
matter? Would you mind getting up? You are
sitting on my front door."

Anna looked up in surprise. A tiny creature
with long, pointed wings, pointed ears, and
pointed shoes stood beside her.

"Are you a pixie?" asked Anna, in
astonishment. "Am I really sitting
on your front door? I'm so sorry."
She got up, and saw that she
was sitting on a small yellow
trap door, half hidden by
fallen leaves.

"Why are you crying?" the pixie asked.

Anna told him all about the little pram she had found, and how it had run off with her doll.

"Oh, that pram belongs to Mother Dimity, the Old Woman Who Lives In A Shoe," said the pixie. "She is very forgetful, you know, and leaves it about everywhere! If she goes home without it, all she has to do is whistle for it and it will run home on its own."

"Well, it's taken my doll too," said Anna, beginning to cry again.

"Please don't do that," said the pixie. "You are making my home all damp. Anyway, you can easily find your doll. Mother Dimity will give her back if you ask her nicely."

"But where does she live?" asked Anna.

"Why, in the Shoe of course," said the pixie. "Knock at the Big Oak Tree six times, go down the steps and find a boat to take you on the Underground River. Then ask the Wizard Who Grows Toadstools where the Shoe is. He is sure to know, because the Old Woman is his sister."

"Thank you," said Anna, getting up. The pixie said goodbye and shut his trapdoor with a bang, leaving Anna to look for the Big Oak Tree.

Anna waited for a little while to see if anyone came, but nobody did. Then she began to wonder. Would it matter if she wheeled Victoria about in the pram for five minutes? Surely it would do no harm. So Anna picked up her doll and strapped her in. She set the soft pillow up behind her so that she could sit up comfortably and tucked the white cover round her legs.

But as she was about to wheel her around the little wood, Anna thought she saw a little pointed face peeping at her from behind a tree.

Anna soon found a large oak tree. She knocked on it, but nothing happened. Then she saw the biggest oak tree she had ever seen in her life!

"That's the one!" thought Anna, and she ran over to it. She knocked on the trunk sharply six times – rat-tat-tat-tat-tat-tat! Then there came a creaking noise, and to her delight a small door swung open in the tree. A narrow flight of steps led downwards through the roots.

Anna slipped through the door, which at once shut with a bang, and began to go down the steps. It was rather dark, but small lanterns hung here and there giving a little light. Anna climbed down a long way.

Eventually she came to a wide passage, with a row of doors on each side. She looked closely at them. Each door had a name on it , or a message, written on a little white card.

The first card said: "Please ring, don't knock." The second said: "Please knock, don't ring." And the third door had a card that said: "Please don't knock or ring." As if that wasn't enough, the fourth door said: "I am not at home yesterday or tomorrow."

Anna thought that was very strange, and she giggled. The doors also had names on them and they were strange too.

"Mister Woozle" was on one card, and "Dame High-come-quick" was on another. Anna decided to walk straight on, and at last she heard the sound of lapping water.

"That must be the Underground River," she thought, pleased. "Now I must find a boat!"

She soon came to the riverbank. It was hung with fairy lights of all colours and looked very pretty. There were plenty of boats on the side of it, but none of them had oars. Anna looked about for someone to row her down the river, but she could see no one.

"Is there anyone here?" she shouted. Then a furry head came poking out of a funny little ticket-office that Anna had not noticed.

"Yes, I'm here, and you're here too," said the voice from the ticket office. Anna went up and saw a grey rabbit with a collar round its neck, and a spotty tie, very neatly knotted.

"Good morning," said Anna. "I would like to borrow a boat."

"Here's your ticket, then," said the friendly rabbit, handing her a very chewed-looking piece of cardboard.

"How much is it?" asked Anna.

"Oh, nothing!" he replied cheerily. "Everything is free here!"

"Where's the boatman?" asked Anna.

"Nowhere," said the rabbit. "There isn't one."

"Then how can I go anywhere?" asked Anna.

"Climb in," said the rabbit, "and the boat will take you."

Anna frowned at the rabbit, and walked up to one of the boats. She chose a blue one, dotted with gold stars, and climbed into it. At once the boat set off by itself.

It shot on down the river, and after a little while it left the underground tunnel and came out into the open air. The boat sped on and on, and Anna saw with surprise that the surrounding fields were full of animals dressed up like human beings.

Suddenly Anna saw a curious sight. In the middle of a field stood a strange-looking old man waving a stick about. He was surrounded by toadstools of all sizes, colours and shapes, and she guessed that he must be the Wizard Who Grows Toadstools.

"Stop, stop!" she cried to the boat. It stopped at once and headed towards the bank. Anna patted the boat, said thank you and then jumped out. She went up to the old wizard. He didn't see her at first and almost knocked her over with his silver wand.

"Please," she said. "I've come to ask you where your sister, the Old Woman Who Lives In A Shoe, is. I want to go and speak to her."

"You'll find her on the other side of that hill," said the wizard, waving his wand violently. "Look out! You are standing just where my next toadstool is growing!"

Just then Anna felt the earth pushing up under her feet. A big toadstool appeared right beneath her. It was covered with big red spots.

"Thank you," said Anna and ran out of the field as quickly as she could. She made her way to the hill in the distance. She climbed it, and as soon as she came to the top she saw the Shoe.

It was enormous, and it had windows and doors and a chimney at the top. Anna thought it looked lovely. She ran down to it, and at once she was surrounded by a crowd of small pixie children, with pointed faces, pointed ears and short wings.

"Who are you? Where do you come from?" they cried in excitement. "Have you come to see our new child?"

"You can see her through the window!" said a tiny pixie, taking Anna's hand and leading her to a window. Anna peeped in – and there, in the bed nearest the window, lay Victoria, her very own doll!

"She arrived today in Mother Dimity's pram," explained the pixie. "But she won't talk, or eat, or drink. She won't even blink her eyes!"

"That's because she isn't a little girl at all," cried Anna. "She's my doll and her name is Victoria!"

"A doll!" said the pixie children, crowding round Anna. "What's a doll? We don't know what a doll is."

"Well, a doll is – a doll is – well, that's what a doll is!" said Anna, pointing to where Victoria lay on the little bed.

"But can't the poor thing move or talk at all?" asked the pixies in surprise.

"Of course not," said Anna and she ran in through the door of the big Shoe, and bumped into the Old Woman.

"Now then, gently, gently!" said Mother Dimity. "You'll frighten the new little girl, rushing about like that. I've just given her some very strong magic medicine to make her come alive again."

"She never has been alive!" cried Anna. "She's my doll!"

"Your doll!" said the Old Woman. "Oh goodness! I remember once seeing a doll in the Land of Boys and Girls. Well, she looks a lot like a little girl, don't you agree? And she'll be even more like one now that I've given her the medicine."

"Do you mean to say that Victoria will be able to walk and talk?" cried Anna.

"Of course," said Mother Dimity. "Look – she is blinking her eyes now! Perhaps I had better change her back into a doll again."

"No, please don't," said Anna at once. She ran to Victoria and looked at her. The little doll was opening and shutting her eyes and she suddenly looked at Anna and smiled a wide smile, showing all her pretty teeth.

"Hello," she said. "I've often wanted to talk to you, and now I can!"

"Oh, what fun we'll have together now!" Anna cried, hugging her doll to her. "We can talk to one another, and play all kinds of games."

"But you mustn't let any one but yourself know," said Mother Dimity at once. "If you do, the magic will disappear, and Victoria will be an ordinary doll again."

"Oh, I won't tell any one at all!" said Anna, happily. "Come on, Victoria, we'll go home now. It must be getting late."

Mother Dimity showed them a quick way home, and they arrived there just in time for dinner. Anna put Victoria in her cot, and told her to be sure not to move if any one came in, and she promised. And now Anna is as happy as can be, for she has a real, live doll to play with her, and they *do* have some fine games together.

"Really!" Anna's mother often says, "you might think that doll was alive, the way Anna plays with her all day long!"

And then Anna smiles a big smile – but she doesn't say a word! She has a wonderful secret to keep and she keeps it very well!